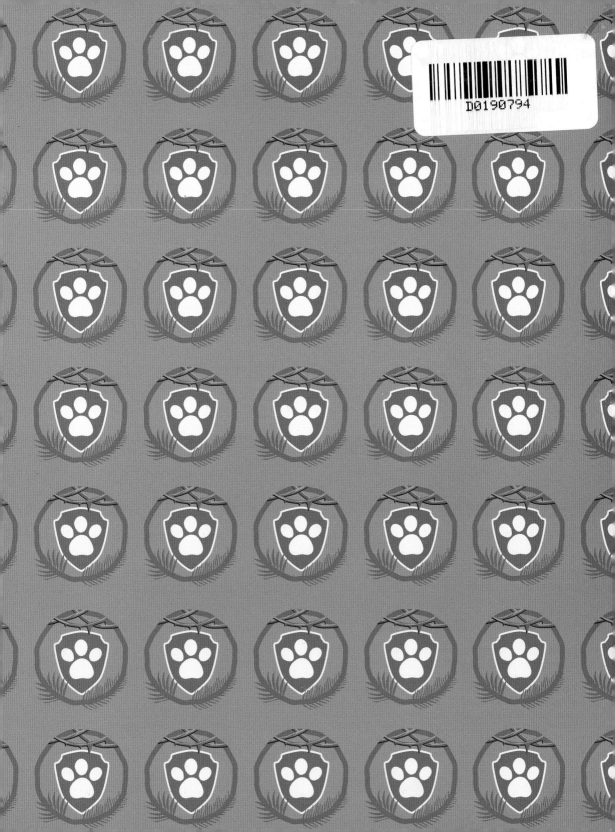

This edition published by Parragon Books Ltd in 2018

Parragon Books Ltd
Chartist House
15–17 Trim Street
Bath BA1 1HA, UK
www.parragon.com

ISBN 978-1-4748-9151-6

Printed in China

Meet Tracker

Bath • New York • Cologne • Melbourne • Delhi
Hong Kong • Shenzhen • Singapore

The PAW Patrol's friend Carlos was busy digging for treasure in the jungle.

"I love discovering new things," he said to himself as he worked. "The jungle is a beautiful place, too. I must tell Ryder what a great spot this is."

Ryder was excited to hear about the dig.
"Hey, Carlos! Do you need any help?" he asked
over the PubPad.
"No, I'm fine. I'm having a great time," said Carlos.
"I'll call you as soon as I find treasure!"
"Okay," laughed Ryder. "We'll be ready to roll when
you need us."

As Carlos was chatting he stepped forwards. "Waaah!" he cried.

He had tumbled into a deep hole, and it was too steep for him to climb out! He had dropped his phone, too, but luckily Ryder had seen everything on his PupPad.

"PAW Patrol, to the PAW Patroller!" Ryder said.
"We've got to rumble to the jungle to save Carlos."
The pups raced aboard their rescue vehicles.
But how were they going to find the hole
in the jungle and rescue their friend?
Meanwhile, Carlos was trapped and
he couldn't reach his phone.
He had to shout for help.
"Help! I'm down here!"

Luckily for Carlos and the PAW Patrol, there was a very special dog in the jungle that day. The pup had big ears that helped him to hear noises from a long way away. He picked up the sound of Carlos shouting and raced towards the sound.

The jungle pup soon found the hole.
  "My name is Tracker and I'll do whatever it takes to rescue you," he called to Carlos.
  "I'm trapped! Can you find my phone and give my friends directions to this hole?" asked Carlos.
  "Sí! I'm on it," said Tracker.

Tracker quickly found Carlos's phone. He pressed the screen and it rang through to the PAW Patroller. The pup crew were surprised to see a dog they'd never met before.

"Buenos días. My name is Tracker," he said. "I'll help guide you to the hole where your amigo is trapped."

"Thanks, Tracker. Good to meet you," replied Ryder. "We're on our way."

As Tracker was speaking to the PAW Patrol, a dangerous snake was slithering towards the hole. It was the longest, hungriest, meanest snake in the jungle.

Sssssssssss...

"Hey, Señor Slithery. Back off!" Tracker called as he leaped in front of the scary snake.

Down below in the hole, Carlos could hear Tracker barking.

"That's one brave pup," he said.

The snake wasn't scared away for long.
But the PAW Patrol arrived just in time
to help frighten the snake away for good.
They used the PAW Patroller horn to blast
out noise that made it slither off quickly.
   "The PAW Patrol is on a roll!" cried Ryder
as they raced towards the hole.

Chase used his night-vision goggles to spot Carlos at the bottom of the hole. Then he guided the winch from the back of his vehicle down to Carlos.

"Winch! Retract!" Chase barked, and the winch pulled Carlos up safely.

Finally, Marshall used his X-ray equipment to check that Carlos wasn't hurt.

"I'm fine," he confirmed.

"For being such a brave pup and saving Carlos,
we'd like you to join the PAW Patrol, Tracker," said Ryder.
Tracker was given his very own Pup Pack and
Pup Tag, with a picture of a tracking compass on it.
"I can't wait to see how this all works," he grinned.
"You look awesome," said Marshall.

Rocky showed Tracker how to use the new Pup Pack, and he tried it out.

"Multitool," he barked. Instantly, a robot tool arm slid out from the pack. It had lots of great tools on the end for different jobs.

"Now show everybody your coolest tool," said Ryder.
"Cables!" ordered Tracker.
Zip! Two strong cables with powerful arms slid out of the Pup Pack. Tracker used them to grab a tree branch.

"Now you can swing through the treetops," said Ryder.

"Muchas gracias," cried Tracker and up he went. "What a great view!"

"Wow. Those cables are swinging!" cheered Rubble.

There was one more gift for Tracker as
a reward for his bravery. It was a super-cool
jeep, just right for jungle adventures.
"A jeep? Just for me?" asked Tracker.
"Sí!" cried the pup crew.

"Muchas gracias," said Tracker, "I'm all ears and now I'm all gears, too."

"Welcome to the PAW Patrol," said Ryder. "Get ready to rumble in the jungle with us any time!"

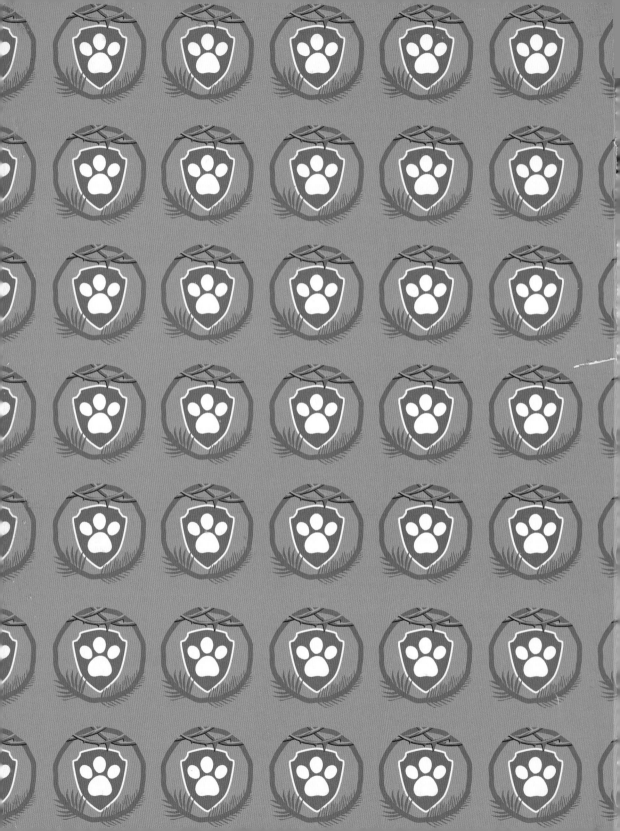